by Bernard Waber

JUST LIKE ABRAHAM LINCOLN

SCHOLASTIC INC.

New York Toronto London Auckland Sydney

ISBN 0-590-43355-5

Copyright © 1964 by Bernard Waber.

All rights reserved. Published by Scholastic Inc.,
730 Broadway, New York, NY 10003, by arrangement with Houghton Mifflin Company.

12 11 10 9 8 7 6 5 4 3 2 1   0 1 2 3 4 5/9

Printed in the U.S.A.   34
First Scholastic printing, January 1990

for Ethel

Mr. Potts, my neighbor, looks just like Abraham Lincoln.

Everyone says so.

Everyone says it's amazing how much
Mr. Potts looks like Abraham Lincoln.

Everyone says Mr. Potts
looks as much like Lincoln
as Lincoln on a penny . . .
maybe even more.

Everyone says
Mr. Potts has
the biggest ears,
the biggest hands,
the biggest feet
and the
kindest heart . . .
just like
Abraham Lincoln.

Everyone says
Mr. Potts has the
saddest eyes . . .
just like
Abraham Lincoln.

Mr. Potts isn't sad. He isn't sad one bit.
Mr. Potts likes to laugh and tell funny stories . . .
just like Abraham Lincoln.

Mr. Potts will help anyone
or anything in need.
It could be a bird with a broken wing.
Mr. Potts will know what to do
to make it better.
He'll set its wing with cardboard and tape.
He'll nurse the bird, bring it food and
watch over it until the wing is mended.

Then he'll take it back to the place where it was found and say, "Fly little bird. You are better. You can fly again."

I like to walk with Mr. Potts.
We talk and we talk.
We talk about trees.
Trees give us paper for books.
Trees give us wood for our furniture and toys.
Trees give us food.

We talk about the sky.
We talk about the sun and clouds.
We talk about what causes rain and snow.
We talk about the wind.

The songs of birds fill our ears.

We talk about Abraham Lincoln.
Young Abe's home was the woodlands.
He wore buckskin breeches, a coonskin cap
and ran barefoot through the wilderness.
Young Abe could hoot like an owl
and hiss like a snake.
We talk and we talk.

2d Edition.

~~[illegible]~~

LEE SURRENDERS

Mr. Potts collects things.
Things like old letters, pictures, maps,
a pair of spectacles, all from
Lincoln's day. He even owns a stovepipe hat
and frock coat just like those worn
by Abraham Lincoln. You can hide secret
messages in a stovepipe. Lincoln did.

Mr. Potts reads every chance he gets . . .
just like Abraham Lincoln. Abraham Lincoln
said, "The things I want to know are in books."
Mr. Potts told me he said it.

Mr. Potts says,
"The poorest
among us can
have books."

Abraham Lincoln was poor.
He walked for miles and miles
to borrow a book, and he
walked for miles and miles
to return it.

Abe took books to the fields
and read while he plowed.
At night he read again by the
light of the fire. In time, he
read just about everything there was
to read for fifty miles around
the Lincoln cabin.

On summer evenings, children
gather around Mr. Potts and
ask to hear stories.
On summer evenings, it is nice to
smell fresh-cut grass, watch
lightning bugs and listen
to stories.

On summer evenings, Mrs. Potts serves
lemonade and cookies, while Mr. Potts
tells stories . . .
stories about Abraham Lincoln.

In school, we have been learning
about Abraham Lincoln.
One day Miss Robin, our teacher, said,
"Our class has been chosen to prepare
an assembly program celebrating
Lincoln's birthday. Would anyone
care to make suggestions?"

"We could tell stories," said one boy.
"We could tell how Abraham Lincoln
was born in a log cabin in Kentucky.
We could tell of the hardships his family
suffered because the soil was poor and
there was little to eat.
We could tell how Abe didn't
even have a real bed and had to sleep
on a mattress of leaves."

"We could tell how Abe helped out
with chores," said another boy.
"We could tell how he carried water
from the spring and kept the woodbox full.
And how, as he grew older, he chopped
down trees to clear the land for planting."

"We could talk about Abe's mother," said a girl. "We could tell how she taught him to be honest and good and to mind his manners."

"We could tell how smart Abe was," said another girl. "We could tell how it wasn't long before he was the best speller in his class."

"I have a suggestion," I said to Miss Robin after class,
"but I have to whisper it."
"And why must you whisper?" she asked.
"So it can be a surprise," I answered . . .
"A wonderful surprise for everyone."
"Very well," she said, "whisper it."
So I whispered it.
Miss Robin smiled.
"That would indeed be a wonderful surprise,"
she said, "and a wonderful experience as well . . .
provided Mr. Potts is willing."

Mr. Potts was willing.
"You could wear your stovepipe
and frock coat," I said.
Mr. Potts tried on the hat and coat.
He looked so much like Lincoln I couldn't
help saying, "If only you had a beard."
"Do you know," said Mr. Potts,
"I've always wanted a good reason
for growing a beard."

It has been said that Abraham Lincoln had
a good reason for growing a beard.
His reason was a letter he received from
a little girl. "How handsome you would look
with a beard!" the little girl wrote.
Abraham Lincoln loved children. He must
have thought it was a good idea too,
for it wasn't long afterwards that he
was wearing a full-grown beard.

Now Mr. Potts has a beard.
It is black with streaks of grey . . .
just like Abraham Lincoln's.

Now people look even more surprised
when they see him.

On the morning of Lincoln's birthday,
Mr. Potts stepped out of his house
dressed in his stovepipe and frock coat
and drove away in a rush.
He had a special appointment . . .
a very special appointment.

"Something most unusual is about to happen," said Miss Robin,
from the school stage. It was later that morning. The Lincoln's
birthday celebration was almost over. "Someone has come,"
she said, "to take us on a journey . . . a magic journey.
He is going to take us back one hundred years, to the town
of Gettysburg. It was there Abraham Lincoln delivered his most
famous speech, the Gettysburg Address. When we arrive we will
hear those very words again."

"Now, in order for the magic to work, it will be necessary for
everyone to close their eyes and keep them closed tight.
When we reach Gettysburg, someone will ask you to open them again.
LISTEN!"

"You may open your eyes now," said
a new voice coming from the stage.
The children opened their eyes and were
astonished at what they saw.
"Welcome to Gettysburg," said a tall,
straight man with the face of Abraham Lincoln.
A buzz ran through the audience.
"It's Abraham Lincoln," cried some.
"It's Mr. Potts," said others, smiling
when they recognized him.
Mr. Potts stepped forward on the stage,
and began to recite the famous speech.
"Fourscore and seven years ago," Mr. Potts began . . .

Suddenly we were in Gettysburg . . .
one hundred years ago, listening to President Lincoln
tell us that America was conceived in liberty
and all men are created equal.
He told us never to forget the brave men who died to
keep us strong and free. And we won't forget.

We won't forget this day, either.

Now Mr. Potts has moved away.
His work has taken him to Washington, D.C.
Mr. Potts is a lawyer . . .
just like Abraham Lincoln.

On the morning of the day Mr. Potts moved,
I rang his doorbell for the very last time.
"Come in," he said. "I have been waiting for you."
I walked in. Packing cases were piled everywhere.
"I have something for you," said Mr. Potts.

I followed him into his study. His bookshelves were
empty now. "I would like you to have the stovepipe," he said,
putting it on my head. The hat was big and covered my eyes.
"One day it will fit you," said Mr. Potts.
"I would also like you to have this book about Abraham
Lincoln's younger years. I have written something on the flyleaf."
"What does it say?" I asked.
"It says, 'To a fellow Lincolnphile.'"
"What does that mean?" I asked.
"It means to someone who admires and is greatly interested
in everything about Abraham Lincoln."

Now Mr. Potts is gone. It took a while getting used to not
seeing him on his porch or walking about
with a book under his long arm.
It took a while getting used to the empty house next door.

But the house isn't empty now.
Someone new is moving in.
Someone named Mr. Pettigrew.

I wonder what he's like.